Experiencing Mr. Luxman

by

James Kenneth Rogers

Published By
ROGERSHAVEN BOOKS

Experiencing Mr. Luxman
by James Kenneth Rogers

Copyright © 2023
by James Kenneth Rogers
All rights reserved.

Inquiries should be addressed to
Inquiries@RogershavenBooks.com

ISBN: 979-8-3304-0861-0

Experiencing Mr. Luxman

Have you ever taken twenty-nine years to finish something? Well, I have—my education. Thirteen years of public school to get my high school diploma. Six years of undergrad (I was having a little too much fun to finish in four). Two years for my master's. Then, I took a few years off to try entrepreneurship. After failing miserably at that, I went back to academics. Four years for my Ph.D. And, finally, four years to do two post-docs and finish my dissertation.

But it was only as I finished all of those twenty-nine years of schooling that I discovered I was never going to be "Professor Cooper."

It wasn't my qualifications. I had degrees from the right schools. I had plenty of publications in peer-reviewed journals. I had great recommendations. And I was a wizard in the lab.

No, everyone had to acknowledge I was a top-rate geneticist. The problem wasn't my resume. It was me.

After a long day of interviewing at a state university in the Midwest, I finally figured it out. My postdoc was almost over, and I was getting desperate for a job as a professor.

My last interview was with an older guy, about to retire—Professor Mitchell. He was the head of the hiring committee. Everything had gone well that day, especially with Professor Mitchell.

At the end of the day, we sat there in his small office, surrounded by shelves filled with books about genetics. He looked like the perfect stereotype of a professor—slightly unkempt grey hair, salt and pepper beard, grey slacks, and a wrinkled button-up white shirt with no tie. I felt right at home. I was thinking that maybe this could be me in thirty or forty years—but with better clothes.

Professor Mitchell and I connected—we had a lot of similar interests, knew people in common, that kind of thing. That was probably why he told me.

"Dr. Cooper, you are a superb candidate," he said. "Any university would be foolish not to snap you up on the spot."

"Gosh, thanks," I said, my hopes rising.

Is he going to make me an offer on the spot? I wondered. *Doesn't the hiring committee have to meet first to decide officially?*

"Which is why I feel I owe you some candor," he said.

Uh oh.

"I'm sorry, but we won't be able to make you an offer," he continued.

I adjusted my collar and cleared my throat. I had *not* been expecting this. Not today.

"May I ask why not?"

"Like I said, it has nothing to do with your qualifications— those are fantastic. It's just that, well, the DIE Committee—"

"DIE Committee?" I interrupted.

"Yes, the Diversity, Inclusion, and Equity Committee. They're breathing down our necks. We haven't been meeting 'expectations' in hiring. You just don't tick any boxes that would allow us to hire you."

I didn't know what to say. We sat in silence for a moment.

"Actually, there *may* be something," Professor Mitchell said, perking up. "You never mentioned a significant other. If you were, well, *you know* . . . "

"Well, uh, I'm single right now. My *girlfriend* just broke up with me. Said she needed to 'find herself.' She's been backpacking across Europe the last few months."

I felt a knot in my stomach. I had tried to forget those first weeks after the breakup and her escape to Europe. Almost every day, she would post new pictures of herself partying with a new guy in a new country. That was what had finally led me to delete all my social media accounts.

I *had* recently just met a new girl, Martha. She was this pretty blond, blue-eyed girl I'd literally run into at the bookstore. We'd hit it off right away, but I was taking it slow. After the emotional trauma of my ex's EuroTrip, I had to be sure before I'd commit to anyone. So, Martha was *definitely* not my girlfriend. Yet.

"Oh, uh, well, too bad, I'm sorry," Professor Mitchell said.

I couldn't tell if he was sorry about the breakup or that my significant other had been a girlfriend.

"Well, they're not really allowed to ask intrusive questions about your personal life," he went on. "It's all based on self-report, you know. If you just sort of fudged things, told them that your preferences were changed or you liked both, or . . . "

"I'm not going to lie about myself just to get a job," I said. I was so mad my hands were shaking. I clenched them to make them stop. I got up. "Thank you for your time, Dr. Mitchell."

I reached out and shook his hand, but what I wanted to do was punch him in the face. Coward. I could tell that he knew this was wrong. He probably just didn't want to speak up and draw a target on his own back—he probably didn't want to lose his university pension.

Later, after I had had time to cool down, I was grateful for Professor Mitchell. At least he had the guts to tell me the truth. I eventually even sent him an email thanking him for his frankness.

Until then, I had been turned down at five universities, but not even my conversation with Professor Mitchell could stop me. I kept pounding the pavement. However, after interviews at ten more universities, I had to face reality: I was *not* going to get hired in academia.

It had been a year since my last postdoc had ended and a year since I had been forced to move back home. My parents were pressuring me to move out and get a job—*any* job—but I was *not* going to become the most overqualified burger-flipper in the history of McDonald's. So, I started a desperate search for *some* kind of genetics job in the private sector.

That's how I came to work for Garridan Luxman of Orbuculum Technologies. I had heard rumors through the grapevine that Orbuculum was involved in something big, a secret genetics project. A friend from my first postdoc knew someone at the company, and he got me an interview there.

The first half of the day was different from my previous job interviews at universities—no one asked about my dissertation and research interests, since the interviewers were tech company managers and not geneticists. The last interview was the only one I even had with a geneticist. He only had a master's degree, but at least he knew enough to talk shop and seemed impressed with my credentials.

Lunch went well, too. Some of the company managers I had interviewed with earlier took me to lunch at the cafeteria. We had a great conversation. I had learned to do a lot of coding for my genetics projects, so we had lots to talk about, geeking out on tech stuff like Linux and Python and R and things like that.

We ate at the Orbuculum cafeteria. Well, the word "cafeteria" doesn't do it justice. It was decked out like a fancy, futuristic-looking Starbucks. And the food was just amazing—there were so many options, and it was all so *good*. A foodie could have eaten there every day for months on end and still had something new to delight his palate. I was starting to think that maybe working in the private sector wouldn't be such a bad idea. I was curious, though, about one thing,

"I'm surprised that the cafeteria has so many meat options available," I said. "I mean, not that I'm complaining or anything, this barbecue sandwich is amazing. But I thought Garridan Luxman was a vegetarian."

"Well, that's not quite right," one of the managers explained. "He eats meat, but only from animals he's killed himself. He said he thinks it's more ethical—that you shouldn't be willing to eat anything you haven't killed yourself."

"Oh, how interesting," I said, nodding, while thinking the guy was kind of a weirdo.

The conversation turned back to tech stuff after that. What I really wanted them to talk about, though, was the new genetics project at Orbuculum. So far, no one had told me what it was even about. When I first heard that Orbuculum was starting a genetics project, I assumed that they were going to launch some kind of new genetics at-home kit to check your ancestry and health issues. And that was why I hadn't been too interested in jobs in the private sector in the first place. DNA test kits that were direct-to-consumer—"DTC" as we usually called it—were boring 15-year-old technology. I wanted to work on the cutting edge. When I was trying to become a professor, my ambition had been to set up my own lab and give David Reich a run for his money.

In the days leading up to my interview, I had done some due diligence to learn more about Orbuculum, hoping to figure out what I might be getting into in a job at a place like that. I was as puzzled as ever, though. Orbuculum entering the DTC genetics market didn't make much sense. There were already several successful companies that did stuff like that, and when Orbuculum wanted to get into a new market segment, it usually just bought another company that was already in that space. That was how Orbuculum had become such a big player in social media—it had purchased several big social media sites, combined them, and then used its money and power to promote its new social media

Frankenstein and make it grow even bigger. It had done something similar with online video streaming. If it wanted to get into genetics, why wouldn't it just buy a genetics company, too?

So, throughout lunch, I tried to fish for more information, but the guys with me wouldn't take the bait. Or, I realized toward the end of lunch, maybe they just didn't know what the project was.

It was after lunch when things started to get more unusual. The first thing they did after I got back from the Orbuculum cafeteria was give me an IQ test.

I had never been asked to take an IQ test as part of a job application. In fact, the more that I thought about it, I was pretty sure that IQ tests were illegal. Didn't some court decision find that they were racist or something? But I needed the job, so I took the test.

After I finished, they sent me to a waiting room and told me they'd call me back in a few minutes. The Orbuculum waiting room had a nice video game set up and a pool table. I didn't feel like playing anything, though. I was too nervous. I *really* needed this job. Martha and I had been getting more serious. But how could I ask someone to marry me when I was still living at my parents' house? So, I just sat on one of the leather recliners and waited.

"Cooper?" the receptionist called a few minutes later. "Paul Cooper?"

I got up and went over to her desk. A young man was standing behind her in the doorway. He looked like a male model —square shoulders and jaw, perfect hair, and dressed in a very expensive-looking Italian suit.

"Yes, that's me," I said.

"Dr. Cooper," the young man said, extending his hand. "My name is Brian Scarpello. I'm Garridan Luxman's personal assistant. He'd like to meet you.

"Wow," I responded, shaking his hand. "Thank you!"

That got my hopes up. The billionaire himself wanted to meet me? Apparently, I must have gotten a good score on the IQ test.

"But, first, we'll need you to sign an NDA, please," Brian said.

"NDA?"

"Yes, a non-disclosure agreement. It's a standard thing in the industry. Just promising you won't disclose anything you're about to hear."

He handed me a stack of papers. It was thick. I started flipping through it, trying to read over what they wanted me to sign. The print was small, and it was at least 100 pages long.

"Of course, feel free to read it if you want to," Brian said. "But unless you have a law degree from Harvard and about ten years' experience in IP and employment law, it probably won't make any sense to you. Would you like me to translate?"

"Uh, OK."

"This has been drafted by some of the best lawyers in Silicon Valley. Ironclad. Enforceable in all fifty states and most of the rest of the civilized world as well. You're promising you'll never disclose what you're about to discuss with Mr. Luxman to *anyone*. And during employment, you can't talk about your work to anyone. Not even after leaving your job. Not ever."

Signing this thing sounded pretty serious. That worried me a little, but it aroused my curiosity even more. What was this all about?

And the way he was talking about confidentiality during employment. That got my hopes up. Maybe things would work out after all. Maybe I could marry Martha and settle down.

Brian led the way down a maze of corridors. We passed lots of cubicle farms full of people hard at work on their computers. And we passed the break rooms, which were even better-stocked with amusements than the waiting room, and with lots of free drinks and snacks too.

Finally, we reached an elevator at the end of one of the corridors. Brian scanned an ID card and then pushed the button for the top floor. When we got off, it was like I was in a different building. We stepped out onto plush red carpet. The walls were covered in dark mahogany paneling. Oil paintings hung every ten feet.

"That one's a Monet," Brian said after he noticed me looking at one of the paintings. "And that one's a Picasso. Titian. El Greco. . . ."

It was all very impressive. The cost of any one of those paintings, I was sure, was enough to pay off all my student loans, with enough left over to buy me a nice house and pay for my retirement.

At the end of the corridor was a set of double doors. There were carved wood panels on each door. As we got closer, it looked like most of the panels had carvings showing scenes from Garridan Luxman's life. I tried to look at as many as I could. The first one showed him at boarding school in Darwin, Australia—a man stood at the head of a classroom, towering over a young Garridan. The next one showed his family moving to the United States. One showed him sitting at a computer (presumably coding the first Orbuculum database software). There were a lot of carvings depicting him having different adventures as an adult. My favorite was the one showing him getting launched into space on a rocket from VirgoPoint, his rocketry company. Only the top half of the doors' panels had carvings. The rest were all blank.

Brian scanned his ID badge again and opened the door on the left side.

We entered Garridan Luxman's "office." It was about 2,000 square feet. It was full of antique furniture, and the wall was filled with oil paintings worthy of a world-class art museum.

At the other end of the room, sitting at a desk that looked like it would have been right at home in the Oval Office, was Garridan Luxman himself. He was in his mid-50s. The man didn't match the office. He was dressed in a wrinkled polo and khaki slacks. He had dark brown eyes and an aquiline nose. His receding hairline gave him a big forehead, and his unkempt brown hair was turning gray in a few places. He was slouched in his seat, typing something on his computer.

"Doctor Cooper!" he said, standing and coming around the front of his desk. "Welcome! Thank you for coming."

He extended his hand as I approached. We shook.

"Pleased to me you, Mr. Luxman," I said. "But, please, just call me Paul."

"Good to meet you too," he said. "And you can call me Garridan. Please, have a seat."

He motioned to a nice leather seat in front of his desk.

I sat. I looked around for Brian, but he had disappeared.

"So, how has your day been here with us?" he asked.

"Wonderful, I've had a great experience so far," I said.

"*Experience.* I like that word. You know, at my stage in life, after getting enough money to buy any *thing* I want, what I've learned, is that it's the *experiences* that count more."

"Uh, yeah, I agree. But as a poor post-doc, I'd have to say that money sure doesn't hurt either."

Mr. Luxman laughed.

"Indeed, indeed," he said. "And that is why we are perfect for each other. You have the expertise and knowledge that I so desperately need, and I have, well . . . Paul, I'm sure you've been wondering what this project is all about."

"Yes, as a matter of fact, I had. My first thought was DTC genetics kits or something, but that doesn't—"

"Make any sense for Orbuculum?" Mr. Luxman interrupted. "You're absolutely right. Paul, as you can imagine, I'm a busy man, but this project is very important to me. So let me just come right out and say what it's about: dinosaurs."

"Dinosaurs?"

"Or, rather, dinosaur. Singular. One of them."

"What do you mean?" I asked.

"Six months ago, something exciting was discovered on an island off the coast of Antarctica. Something that should have been impossible. A frozen dinosaur."

I couldn't believe what I was hearing. Even for someone as rich as Mr. Luxman, that was impossible, wasn't it?

"What?" was all I could manage to say.

"Or rather, a tiny fragment of a frozen dinosaur," he added. "But it's not just bone. There's flesh. And, we hope, DNA."

"How is that possible?" I asked. "Are you sure?

"I've had the best experts on this," he said. "I've kept it very hush-hush, of course. I've only made targeted inquiries to different experts, so none of them knows the whole picture of what I have. But I've asked a lot of questions of a lot of people, and at this point, I'm sure. Most likely, it's a previously unknown species of theropod. It wouldn't have been very big—probably weighed somewhere between five and twenty pounds and was maybe between one and three feet tall. But a small dinosaur is fine for my purposes. Perfect, really. Not too big to go all 'velociraptor' on us."

"So, you're trying to pull off a real-life Jurassic Park?" I asked. "Resurrect dinosaurs for some kind of a theme park?"

I was sitting on the edge of my seat now. The idea of making a real-life Jurassic Park seemed a bit over-the-top to me. But, on the other hand, if what Mr. Luxman was saying was true—if they really had a piece of frozen dinosaur flesh. Well, that would be the chance of a lifetime for *any* geneticist, let alone an unemployed one.

"Yes, on the resurrection part," Mr. Luxman said. "No, on the theme park. I have no aspirations to be Walt Disney or to run a zoo. Paul, sometimes, when an opportunity presents itself, you have to take it and then figure out what to do about it later. That's what we're going to do here. I want you to worry about bringing that dinosaur back from the dead. You let me worry about what to do about it once you do."

"Yeah, about that," I said. "I'm not so sure about what you've got here. There is no way a frozen dinosaur could have survived intact for 60 million years. Not even just a piece."

"I never said it was 60 million years old," he said. He paused. "Don't get me wrong, it *is* ancient, just not that old. But my paleontologists are *very* sure that this is from a real dinosaur. They think it was from a relict population that must have survived on that island after the rest of the dinosaurs went extinct."

"Have you done any DNA analysis yet?" I asked.

"Only the very basics—that's where you come in," Mr. Luxman said. "I want to hire you because you are an expert in extracting ancient DNA from archeological samples, right?"

"Well, yes," I said. "That is one of the things I specialized in."

"And after you finished your master's degree, you and your friends created an animal cloning startup, right?"

"Yeah," I said sheepishly. "We cloned peoples' dead pets. But the company failed, and I realized that it wasn't really something I wanted to specialize in—"

"Well, I want to keep this project extremely confidential," Mr. Luxman said. "Which means having the absolute minimum number of people working on it. So I need someone to head this up who can wear many hats, such as doing both DNA extraction and cloning. Is that something you'd be capable of?"

I paused. I was a little rusty on the cloning, but not *that* rusty. And ancient DNA extraction? On that, I was an ace.

"Yes," I answered confidently.

"Then, can you head up my efforts to extract the DNA and clone the dinosaur?"

Well, how could I say no? If Mr. Luxman was full of it, at least I'd be bringing in a paycheck and get to work on the best lab equipment money could buy.

And if he was telling the truth, well, then this was the opportunity of a lifetime. I had gone from being an unemployable loser to having dreams of a possible Nobel Prize.

So, I accepted the job. The work itself was great, but the secrecy was frustrating. Brian hadn't been kidding about that NDA. I couldn't tell *anyone* about what I was working on. But my mom and dad didn't much mind—they were just happy that I moved out.

It didn't take long for me to do my own tests to confirm that Mr. Luxman really had a piece of frozen dinosaur. At first, I thought six months was all it would take to do this project, one way or the other—to either crack the problem or prove that what Mr. Luxman wanted wasn't possible.

But these kinds of things have a way of taking on a life of their own and then going way longer than you thought they would. It took a lot of work to figure out the technical details. No one had ever worked with a sample this old before. I had to invent whole new methods of DNA recovery, amplification, and imputation. Then, after all of that, I had to figure out the nuclear transfer issues.

Since this project was so hush-hush, our teams were tiny, and most of the time, I worked alone. I missed having other people around to bounce ideas off of. I think Mr. Luxman, his assistant, and I were the only people who knew what we were really working on.

But at least I had the best equipment money could buy, or more and more often, the best equipment that money could *build*, as I had to make a lot of it myself. Money was no object. Mr. Luxman essentially gave me a blank check.

The funny thing was, though, after that first day, I didn't deal with Mr. Luxman anymore. I guess he was too busy running Orbuculum and having more of his "experiences," like the time the tabloids published photos of him playing golf on top of Everest, or the time he set the world record for the deepest human submarine dive into the Mariana Trench.

I still had to give weekly progress reports on the work, but always to Mr. Luxman's assistants. Every year, he got a new assistant. After Brian, it was Peter, then Micah, then Abraham, then Jeremy.

Time passed. And while I made glacially slow progress with the project, at least I *was* making progress. In other areas of my life, not so much. Martha and I broke up. She told me she just wasn't ready to settle down—didn't want to feel like she was missing out on the rest of her twenties.

I gained a nephew, at least. My older sister had a baby boy. She named him Henry after her father-in-law. He was a cute kid, and it was nice getting to spend time with him and the rest of my family.

But mostly, I spent my time working.

And finally, four and a half years after I started, my work paid off. We had an honest-to-goodness dinosaur egg. It spent several weeks of careful tending under the incubator, with just about every kind of sensor you can imagine monitoring the embryo's development inside. Then, finally, the dinosaur hatched.

Hatching day was the first time I had seen Mr. Luxman since my interview. He was ecstatic. And so was I, of course. I was already planning my Nobel Prize acceptance speech.

Mr. Luxman didn't want to name the dinosaur, so I did. One of Henry's favorite picture books was *Danny and the Dinosaur*. So, naturally, I named the dinosaur Danny.

When I got home that evening, I invited my sister's family and Mom and Dad over for dinner. I cracked open a bottle of expensive champagne I'd been keeping for this moment to celebrate. It was maddening to not be able to tell them exactly what the "big breakthrough" was at work, but they said they were happy for me.

Probably no animal in the history of the world had been so meticulously taken care of. Mr. Luxman really spared no expense now. It was amazing seeing this ghost from the past, resurrected and real, in front of me. He was beautiful. He stood on two legs, with a big tail behind him for balance. His feet each had one big talon and then smaller toes. He had scaly green skin that was covered by a thick layer of white feathers, apparently to keep him warm in the Antarctic winters. Along his back, though, was a line of beautiful green feathers. And on his tail, he had a cluster of yellow feathers that he would open up and fan out when he was happy or excited—it looked almost like a small peacock's tail. He had a row of sharp teeth, but he never bit me—just friendly nips now and then. And his face was adorable—like if you took the velociraptors from *Jurassic Park* and crossed them with a puppy.

The funniest part was, it seemed as if he had imprinted on me. Whenever he saw me, he made this adorable cooing noise. I really started to love that little guy. I looked forward to seeing his little head pop up as he heard the lab door open each morning. He would tilt his head and watch me inquisitively through the glass with his big golden eyes as I started my day. It was almost like I had a child of my own.

I hoped, one day soon, to be able to bring Henry and my sister and my mom and dad to come see and be some of the first human beings to ever see a real, live dinosaur. I imagined Henry, smiling and playing with Danny, proud of his uncle and excited to know he was indirectly responsible for choosing the dinosaur's name. It had been so hard never being able to talk about my work with them. I was looking forward to finally being able to tell my family what I had been working on all these years. They'd all been supportive of me, but I could sense a bit of skepticism mixed in, too, when I told them how momentous the project was. For a while, at the beginning, my mom even secretly suspected that I had just gotten a job as a software engineer at Orbuculum and was making up the stuff about working on an important secret genetics project ("important secret genetics project" was the most I could tell them without getting in trouble with Mr. Luxman's lawyers). My dad once even joked with me that I was probably cloning dinosaurs. It was frustrating having to lie and pretend to laugh at the "absurdity" of his joke.

And, of course, I couldn't wait until this all became public. Professor Mitchell and *that* committee would regret not hiring me now!

After about four months, Danny stopped growing. We figured he must have reached adulthood. He was two feet tall and weighed eleven pounds—pretty close to what Mr. Luxman's paleontologists had predicted.

At that point, only four people in the world had seen Danny: Mr. Luxman; his new assistant, Jeremy; a paleontologist they had brought in at my insistence to monitor Danny's growth and health; and, of course, me. I started bothering Jeremy more and more about publicizing our discovery. Clearly, we had proven our success. Danny was the first healthy adult dinosaur in human history. When were we finally going to tell everyone? This kind of news should be shouted from the rooftops.

Then, one day, I went into work, only to discover that Danny was missing from his enclosure. The paleontologist was gone, too. I got frantic. What had happened? Had there been an accident?

Before I could raise too much fuss, Jeremy appeared and told me that Mr. Luxman wanted to see me. Jeremy led the way.

It was the first time I had been invited to Mr. Luxman's inner sanctum since my job interview. But this time, we stopped just outside the carved wooden doors.

"Just a moment," Jeremy said. "Garridan should be finishing up right about now. He'll come out and get us when he's ready."

While we waited, I inspected the carvings on the door. Several panels had been added since my prior visit. The door now showed him golfing on Everest and exploring the Mariana Trench. One panel, though, was clearly brand new. It showed Mr. Luxman seated at his desk, the dinosaur in front of him.

"Hey, well, look at that!" I said to Jeremy proudly. "He's already added the dinosaur to the panel. But maybe your carver should have taken more time. This looks like a rush job. It even looks like Garridan is about to—"

Just then, the door opened. Mr. Luxman stepped out. He had an embroidered silk napkin in his hand. He was wiping his mouth.

"Paul!" he said. "Fabulous work! You really are a wizard. You have my eternal gratitude. Please come in."

He brought me into his office and had me sit on the same leather chair. He sat behind his desk.

"This is for you," he said, sliding over an envelope to me.

I opened it. Inside was a check. There were a lot of zeroes.

"Of course, now that the project is over, I'll have no more need for your services," he said. "Consider this a severance payment. And, a token of my appreciation."

"Wow, Garridan," I said. "I don't know what to say. This is beyond generous. Thank you! But I'm confused. Why would you cancel the project? There's still so much to learn, so much to do. Now that we've proved Danny was able to grow into a viable adult. I think we can really speed up the process to make more follow-up clones. And I've been working on the problem of generating a female. I think I've solved that. I have some ideas on introducing genetic diversity to the mix so we can get a breeding population—"

Mr. Luxman's laugh interrupted my monologue.

"Paul, I admire your enthusiasm, I really do. And I'm sorry to have to tell you that we won't be making any more dinosaurs. No breeding populations."

"But—" I started to say.

"And, I hope you haven't forgotten your nondisclosure agreement. This project is still confidential."

"Why?" I said. "This is something everyone should know about. Why wouldn't you tell anyone?"

I was getting mad now. All those years of work, for what? I could feel that Nobel Prize slipping out of reach.

"Oh, I *will* be telling people," Mr. Luxman said. "But not the public. Just a few of my friends."

"Friends?" I asked. "Why? What's going on? And why wouldn't you want to clone more? Where's Danny?"

"Oh, I do wish you hadn't named him. Just makes it more difficult," he paused and took a breath. "Remember what I said about experiences? Well, I meant every word. That's what I live for. And now I have experienced something that my billionaire friends could only dream of. They're going to be so envious! You see, that's why I can't clone any more dinosaurs. If there were more, then I wouldn't be the only one to experience—"

My heart was starting to sink. I still didn't know what was going on, but I could tell it wasn't good.

"What do you mean, 'experience'?" I interrupted, my eyes narrowing. "Please tell me you mean you're talking about the experience of seeing a real, live dinosaur?"

"Well, that was pretty great, but seeing a dinosaur isn't *that* amazing of an experience. Everyone's watched *Jurassic Park*, after all."

It was then that I noticed a plate on Mr. Luxman's desk. It looked like he had just finished a meal.

He followed my gaze to the plate.

"Now you see, don't you?" he said. "How many people can say they've *eaten* a dinosaur?"

He saw the horror on my face, and he stopped talking for a second.

"Now, Paul, don't worry," he continued. "Danny didn't suffer. I made sure of that. Did it myself. It was quick and pain-less. And even up until the end, I spared no expense. Only the best for our Danny! My chef is world-class. He turned Danny into the world's first and only *dinosaure à l'orange*. Now, *that* was an experience. Tasted like chicken."

What now?

If you enjoyed this story and would like to support James Kenneth Rogers and his fiction you can:

1. Sign up for the email newsletter to get regular updates from James at **JamesKennethRogers/Newsletter**. James's first published full-length novel, *Scouts of the Lost Dutchman*, will be released soon. The book tells the story of three Boy Scouts in Phoenix in 1989 who find the legendary Lost Dutchman's Mine and discover that it contains ancient mysteries--it's like *The Wonder Years* meets *Indiana Jones*. Once it is set for release, the newsletter will be the first place it will be announced.

2. Leave positive ratings or reviews of this story online—it is available for purchase at all major outlets. A short list of places where you can leave reviews is at **JamesKennethRogers/Luxman**.

3. Spread the word by telling your friends about this story and James's fiction.

4. To contact the author or share feedback, send an email to: **Inquiries@JamesKennethRogers.com**.

About the Author

James Kenneth Rogers earned a Juris Doctor from Harvard Law School and a Masters of Law in International Law from the University of Cambridge. A sixth-generation Arizonan, he has lived on four continents. He has four children. His website and blog are at JamesKennethRogers.com.